Contents

Chapter 1
Window

It was forbidden, but Caz had been working on it for weeks now.

And today she would do it.

She'd look out of a window.

It had been very hard to find one. All the walls in Murphy's Department Store were grey and smooth, but in places they were covered with big metal grids that were impossible to move. Caz knew that the windows were behind those grids.

The grid she had chosen was tiny. It was right at the top of the building, in the Toy department. It was in the wall of a small white room and Caz had told everyone that it was her new bedroom. The room had shelves and the door even had a lock that worked. Caz had dragged a bed up here and a dressing-table and all sorts of pictures and mirrors and stuff from the House and Home department. She had propped the pictures and mirrors on the shelves and in bright rows along the floor. Then she'd chosen a new duvet and purple pillows from Bedding.

Every night Caz had worked on the window.

Now she climbed up on a stool and looked at what she had done.

There was a gap in one corner of the window frame where the grey metal grid wasn't fixed well to the wall. Two small rivets held it, and one of those was broken now. It had taken Caz a lot of effort with a screwdriver stolen from the DIY department to do that. Now she attacked the second rivet. She leaned hard into it with the screwdriver, forced it down and swore. Nothing shifted. Caz wiped the sweat from her hands and went at it again. Snap! It broke. She tugged at the grid, bent it back and saw a small corner of dirty glass.

'Look out,' Caz told herself. 'Just look out of the window.'

She was scared.

If Marky found out, he would cut Caz's food ration again. But Caz had spent nine long years locked inside Murphy's Department Store with Marky controlling everything she did. The time had come for her to find out what had happened to the world outside.

She jumped down and checked the door. Safe. She came back and leaned her hands on the wall and put her eye to the window.

Caz looked down. Below her, she saw a street.

At least, it used to be a street. It used to be a high street with shops and banks and tidy buildings and a park with swings and slides. Caz could remember all that.

Now it was a frozen world. Ice covered everything. Street lamps rose from the frost, their bulbs broken and hanging with icicles. Doors and windows were sealed and silent. The park was a spooky tangle of dead trees. Their white branches moved in a fierce wind.

A car lay tipped up on its side. It was frozen deep within the ice and its windows were a web of cracks.

Caz stared in shock. She had expected it to be bad, but not like this. No one could live out there. Then she looked up and saw the sky.

It was blue.

Huge clouds moved across it.

Caz took a breath of wonder. Clouds! She had forgotten how huge and fast clouds were. And the wind! What would it be like to feel the wind on her face? Not to be trapped in the Store with its grey walls and dead air?

Spots of water pattered on the glass.

Rain.

Real rain!

Caz had been five the day the Blue Star had come to Earth. She had been out at the shops, hanging onto Mum's hand in the crowded street. Then the strange icy flakes had flashed down like burning snow, bright and cold and bitter to taste. Caz had laughed and said "Look!" and danced in the strange storm until she had seen how the people around her had started to cough and gasp – choke and die.

Then someone had grabbed her and dragged her into the Store.

And the Store had sealed itself shut.

Why hadn't Caz dragged Mum into the Store with her? Where had Mum gone in that storm of burning snow? Had she survived? These questions kept Caz awake night after night, but she knew the answer. No one on the street could have survived. But Dad had been far off at work in his office down by the river. What about Dad?

The thought of Dad haunted her.

Caz looked back at the frozen street.

She had been afraid that she would see bodies when she looked out. Skulls and bones lying there, bodies gone to rot, clothes worn away to rags.

But if there were bodies they were buried in the ice, lost for ever in this frozen world.

No bodies, no movement.

No birds.

No insects.

And no Blue Star.

The only things to be seen were a few dead leaves gusting in the wind. And as Caz listened to the moan of the wind she realised this was the first sound in nine years that she had heard outside the Store.

Then, just above the icy trees, she saw something. It was far off, tiny. Caz could just hear a metallic humming sound coming from it. It shot across the sky on silver wings. A faint smoky trail spread out behind it and a tiny red light flickered.

Caz was sure she had seen it.

Then it flew behind a far-off building and was gone.

Caz drew back from the window in amazement, then looked again.

The sky was empty.

Could she really have seen that?

A bang on the door made her jump.

"Caz! *Caz!* Are you in there?" a voice called.

Caz almost fell off the stool. Her heart pounded as she turned.

"Caz, didn't you hear the bell? Marky's called another meeting. Everyone's waiting! Come on!" It was Will. His voice was jumpy with fear.

Caz pushed back her hair and unlocked the door. She hoped she didn't look as shocked as she felt.

Will was wearing a white shirt and a pair of dark green trousers from one of the high-end ranges the Store used to sell. He had new leather shoes on too. What's more, Caz could see that they fitted him.

"Where did you get those!" she said, with a sting of envy.

"Found a few things my size in a box in Menswear," Will said. "Maxwell must have been hiding them."

Caz frowned. "You're so lucky!"

"Ah come on, you look all right," he muttered.

She pushed past him, annoyed, because that wasn't true. She had on a mish-mash of stuff – green tights, a purple party dress that she'd been wearing for weeks now, and an old coat belted over it all to keep warm. The coat was stiff with dirt and soon it would be useless. When it was too filthy she'd take it to Fiona in Womenswear and swap it for something new, but all the clothes Caz's size had been used up ages ago. What was left was as frumpy as hell and made for old women twice her size. It was so stupid that in a store full of clothes finding things to wear was such a problem.

If only the washing machines worked!

Will raced off towards the stairs. As Caz raced after him she wanted to tell him to stop, to tell him what she'd done. "Will," she'd say. "Listen! I looked outside. I saw something flying in the sky."

Instead she snapped at him. "Slow down! What's the big rush anyway?"

Will ran down the steps of the still escalator, to Furnishings and its musty heaps of soft, rotting carpets.

At the bottom he turned and looked up at her. "Marky wants another Sacrifice."

"What!" Caz stopped and stared at him. "But Rose ..."

"Rose was a month ago. Things are worse now."

Caz was quiet for a moment, then the sudden clang of the alarm bell made her jump as it burst out.

"That's two already," she whispered. "How many more will he kill?"

Will turned, his face pale. "Maybe all of us, in the end."

Chapter 2

Store

Thirty-one people had survived the Blue Star.

Thirty-one people had lived in Murphy's Department Store.

On the day of the Star Storm, most of them had been shoppers in the Store. A few worked there. Others, like Will, crawled in off the street in the chaos before the shutters crashed down and the airlocks switched on. Murphy's had been fitted with the very latest kit to protect it from terrorist attacks using gas and bombs.

Thirty-one people.

A scared, lost, unhappy community. But they had survived in the Store, with food and air and water and clothes and bedding.

They had argued and tried to get on. They had organised themselves and looked out for one another. They had made a sort of life here.

But that sort of life came to an end when the food started to run out.

Lewis Jackson had been the first Sacrifice.

He was a quiet man. He never joined in the hunts and games and parties. Never argued about his share of the water or where he slept. Never said much at all, but Caz remembered that one time he'd told her about his family and showed her a grimy photo of his wife and two little boys splashing in the waves on a day at the seaside.

He was the first to be chosen.

And then, last month, big cheerful Rose. Rose, who'd cried and struggled in fear as they dragged her away.

Who would be next?

Will caught Caz's elbow. "Come on! Hurry up!" he hissed. "You don't want to make Marky angry. He already thinks you're trouble."

"Wait, Will," Caz said. "Listen! I need to tell you something …"

But Will had already run along the messy aisles of House and Home and out into the space they used as a meeting hall.

Caz had no choice but to follow. Her stomach churned with dread. That was even worse than the hunger. And she was always hungry now.

Cosmetics had been the biggest department, the one right at the front of the shop. Back then, it was a glittering paradise of bottles and mirrors. Even now the glass and marble hall still stank of perfume and aftershave, soap and body lotion. Most of that useless stuff was now stacked in boxes against the walls or piled under the counters that they had shoved together to make space.

In the middle there was a grubby collection of chairs and sofas and stools.

The Store's residents sat on the chairs, in a buzz of worried talk.

Caz and Will were by far the youngest. Mrs Price was the eldest – she had been 70 last year. The rest were in between. There were 20 women and 11 men. Or there had been.

Maxwell ran Menswear just as he had done before the Blue Star. Fiona, who had been a hairdresser back then, ran Womenswear.

Food was the most vital department. Whoever ran Food ran the Store. There had been arguments over it from the start, but Marky held it now. Marky was the boss.

Marky was thin, with a smooth face and a permanent smile. The only reason he'd been in the Store on the day the Star came was that Maxwell had just nabbed him for shoplifting. Caz didn't trust Marky. None of them did. But somehow, over the last few years, Marky had made himself leader. In the early days there had been votes. Maxwell had been in the army as a young man, and he had made speeches about committees and rotas and how they should be fair.

But that was years ago. Maxwell was half-starved and desperate now, and no one cared about committees and Marky made all the big decisions. Marky controlled the food.

Marky and the Triplets.

Caz watched Marky pull a table over and climb up on it. She snatched a look round at the rest of the group. Marky's girl, Stella, stared back at her in scorn. Stella had been on the till on the day of the Star. She had the best clothes and she was the only one who bothered with make-up now – her sharp, pretty face was caked in it and her nails were painted in delicate stripes of blue and purple. Caz could see that she'd made Fiona style her blonde hair in layers of big curls.

Caz looked away from Stella and at Marky's sidekicks. They'd planted themselves like soldiers around the table Marky was standing on. They were real triplets – identical brothers – big and bald and fierce. There was no point in even thinking about crossing them. The Triplets followed Marky like dogs. He was the brains. They were his weapons. The food stores were going down all the time, but the Triplets and Marky and Stella always seemed to have plenty to eat.

And now things were going to get worse.

"So, people," Marky said. His face was grim. "It's been a month since Rose left us. We all know how hard that was. Her bravery, her guts ... a huge example to us all."

Silence.

Will looked at Caz.

They knew what was coming.

Marky put his hands in his pockets. He looked round. "This morning we took stock of the food again. The tinned supplies are down to thirty cases and there's even less of the dried stuff. The deep freezes are still half full, but the generator is on its last legs. Naz reckons it won't last another month."

Caz frowned. Marky had said that last time. The generator was in the basement and it was their only source of power. It was old but it still worked. Naz pretty much lived by its side. If the generator went down, then the heat and light and air in the Store would go with it.

She thought again of the flying object. How it had shone silver. The flickering red light.

It had been real.

People must have made it. *There must be people, alive, out there somewhere.*

"So I'm afraid," Marky said, "that we're faced with another terrible choice. We have to make another Sacrifice. For the good of the group."

There was a murmur of voices, of protest, but it was so mild that it faded almost before it began. Marky had them so weary now, Caz thought, so broken and cowed. In the early days, people would have stood up, yelled, shouted. Not any more. Not with the Triplets in a solid row behind Marky.

Marky held up a hand. "We have to draw lots to find out who goes next," he said. "That's only fair. It could be me, it could be you. Complete random choice. But whoever it is will be giving their life for the group."

He turned. "Bring the papers, Stell."

It wouldn't be him. Everyone knew that the draw was rigged. It had to be. The two who had already gone – Lewis and Rose – had been Marky's biggest enemies and he'd got rid of them first. He'd hated Lewis for how Lewis had looked at Marky with his dark, clever eyes and pointed out the flaws in Marky's plans with just a word or two. And Rose got on his wrong side with her energy and kindness – she'd set up the games and parties in the early days, and Marky couldn't stand how the fun she created made people like each other more.

Stella carried over a small glass vase. Inside it were pieces of paper, already folded up. One for each of them.

Marky held the vase up. "One of these 29 pieces of paper is marked with a black cross. Whoever gets it is the Sacrifice. Whoever gets it leaves the Store. It's tough, but it has to be done."

He jumped down off the table and walked to Fiona and held out the vase. Her face was even paler than usual and as she stretched out her hand it trembled with fear.

Caz couldn't stand it a moment longer.

"*Wait!*" she said.

Fiona's fingers stopped. Everyone looked at Caz.

"Why does it have to be one person?" Caz said. Her voice shook and she felt her face flush hot and angry. "Why don't we all go? Why don't we take the grids down and look out, see what's out there. It might be …"

"We know what's out there." Maxwell spoke from the back. "Air we can't breathe, the whole city a frozen place of death. Wild animals prowling in packs ..."

"How do you know?" Caz snapped.

"What?"

"How do you know?" she repeated. "That there are animals ..."

"Because we hear them, Caz!" Maxwell said. "You know that!"

They all stared at her in astonishment. But she couldn't stop now. All her doubts came tumbling out.

"Maybe we're wrong," she said. "Maybe the howls we hear and those weird cries aren't animals. Maybe it's the ice, moving. Maybe people – other people – have survived out there. Maybe there are other groups like ours."

They stared at her so hard that she thought for a moment she might have convinced them.

But then Marky turned his thin face to her and smiled a sad smile. "So why haven't Lewis or Rose come back to tell us about it then?" he said. "Explain that, Caz."

Chapter 3
Sacrifice

Caz didn't have an answer to that. She didn't know what had become of Lewis or Rose.

Behind her, Will grabbed her arm. "Shut up!" he hissed.

"It's just a dream you have, Caz." Marky smiled at her with oily kindness. "I understand. We'd all love it to be like the old days, wouldn't we? But out there, when you open that airlock and leave, you're in a world of radiation and disease. Who knows what the Star rained down? No one could have survived. We were lucky. This Store was built to withstand bombs and fire, and it was stacked to the roof with supplies. But in ordinary shops and offices and houses, everyone died. They must have. There was nothing to keep them alive."

Caz looked at him. He had folded his arms, pleased with his speech. She wanted to wipe the smug smile off his face, shout out that she had broken the rule, that she had looked outside and seen that light in the sky. But she knew it was safer to keep her mouth shut.

"So." Marky turned back to Fiona. "Let's start. The sooner we start, the sooner we all know."

Fiona blew hair from her eyes. She was white with fear but she stuck her hand in and brought out a piece of paper. She opened it, then held it up.

It was blank.

Her whole body sagged with relief.

Marky took the vase to Naz, then Ade, then Gwen. They each pulled out a blank piece of paper.

"And just to show you it's all fair I'll pick now." Marky smiled, pulled one out and held it up. "Blank."

Caz hissed in disbelief. Will pulled her to one side. "Are you mad? Don't let him think you're trouble!"

"He already does."

"Yes, but be careful! We know the draw is rigged. He'd never let it be him, or Stella, or the Triplets. It's not random. He chooses."

Caz knew that. But she felt wild with anger – bitter and reckless. "I don't care!" she said. "I'm sick of taking orders from him. I'm sick of hiding and being so scared. I'm sick of the Store."

Will stared at her. Before he could say anything they realised that everyone was looking at them.

Marky was holding the glass vase out. Half the papers were gone.

"Your turn." Marky smiled at Caz, and his eyes were blue and hard.

And she knew that whatever paper she took out it would have the black cross on it.

She froze.

"Scared?" Marky said in a low whisper.

"Should I be?"

He smiled.

She reached out.

But before she could get her fingers inside the glass, Will moved. His hand plunged in first.

"No!" she breathed.

Too late. She saw his fingers grope for a paper. He pulled it out between finger and thumb.

He turned the paper over and looked at it.

Caz saw a large black cross.

One of the Triplets sniggered.

No one moved until Marky spoke. "Now that is a shame," he said. "Bad luck, Will. Tough call."

Will nodded. When he spoke, his voice was hoarse. "Better me than someone else," he said.

Will was the only real friend Caz had ever had. She had known him for nine years now. The idea of living here without him was appalling. "I'm coming with you," she blurted.

Everyone stared at her.

"No way!" Will said.

"I am. It's OK. I know it will be OK."

Caz held Will's gaze, trying to tell him that she had seen something out there, something alive.

Maybe something human.

But he only looked more miserable. "I can't let you," he said.

"It's not your choice."

Quick as a thought, Caz put her hand in the glass vase and snatched a paper. She held it tight in her closed fist. Marky's eyes opened wider.

"Shall I open it?" she whispered. "And show everyone? Will there be a black cross on this one too?"

Marky's face was rigid with stress. "Caz," he muttered. "Someone has to run this place."

She smiled and shook her head. "You make me sick," she spat. She threw the paper away, turned her back on him and grabbed Will's arm. "We're better off out of here."

"The Sacrifice is chosen," Marky said. He thrust the vase at Stella, who rushed off with it. Then, with an evil scowl at Caz, he pushed through the group and out of the room.

Caz stood there in a daze as the others came up to hug her and Will, to say how sorry they were, how sad to see them go.

Caz hugged them back. She knew they were sad, but she also knew how glad each of them were that it wasn't them.

Then Caz ran up to her room and threw a few things in a bag. Her heart was racing with terror and excitement. Was she mad? Or was this the best thing she had ever done?

Then she went to find Will.

He was sitting on his tatty king-size bed in Menswear. "We're both going to die out there," he said. He looked up at her and dragged his hands through his hair. "You do know that."

"No I don't," Caz said. "We're not going to die, Will."

"Stop kidding yourself, Caz. The air is full of poison."

"You don't know that." Caz crouched down. "Listen. I've looked out. Out the window in my room."

"*What!*" Will's eyes were round with horror

"I thought I saw a machine," Caz said. "A flying machine."

"Thought? You don't know?"

Caz bit her lip. "No. But listen, Will! People always believe what they're told. Marky knows that. But what if the people who tell us stuff don't know any more than we do? What if they're too scared, or too safe, to look? To even look?" She sat next to him. "I saw something flying. Far off. Silver. It might have been a bird, OK, but even if it was, then that means birds can live out there. That means we can too. But I think it was a flying machine. With someone inside."

Will didn't look up.

Not for a long time.

"Then why didn't the others come back and tell us, Caz?" he asked, just as Marky had done. "Why?"

Half an hour later, they both stood at the airlock. The group had been told to stay away. Only

Marky was there, and the Triplets, like a wall behind him.

The airlock was a sleek, silver door.

"Any time you're ready," Caz said.

"You don't seem scared, Caz," Marky said. "As if you know something I don't."

She didn't want him to think that. "Just keeping my chin up." She shrugged and looked away.

Marky looked at Will, who snapped, "Get on with it."

Marky looked over at the nearest of the Triplets, who put his big hand into a slot marked RELEASE and pulled.

With a great crack and shudder, the sealed door opened.

Dust fell from the top and sides of it.

Inside was a dark space.

Caz set her shoulders. She walked in. Will was close behind her.

To her surprise, the Triplet nodded at her. "Got guts, you two," he said.

Then the door slammed and they were in the airlock.

Seconds later, with a crash that made them both jump, the door behind them sprang open. The door to the outside.

Chapter 4
City

The first thing that struck Caz was the terrible cold.

The door had opened out onto a wild, bitter iciness.

And then she noticed other things – strange smells and a thin wailing sound, the sound of the wind as it lifted her hair and stung her face with a frosty touch that made her shiver.

Caz had forgotten what cold was like.

What the wind sounded like.

Will had pulled a black padded coat out of his pack and was tugging it on. Caz saw that his pack was full of climbing kit that he'd stashed away from Fitness. "It's like the time I went into the freezers," he said.

Caz nodded. Then she stepped into the street.

The world opened up. There was no roof above her. She felt exposed – tiny in a vast frozen world.

There was nothing above her. Nothing. It went on for miles and miles. It was the sky. A sky of the palest blue with dots of faint fleecy clouds. She stared up. She wanted to cry out with the weirdness of it.

And on each side, frozen inside great slabs of glassy ice, were the buildings. Some of their doors were shut, others stood open, their windows smashed. The ice held them all tight. Over the years the ice had cracked and moved, so that roofs had fallen, walls had been twisted by its strength.

There was stillness all around them. No sound.

Only the wind wailed in the abandoned city.

"Right," Will said. His voice was an echo in the icy desert. He lifted up the pack. "Let's go."

They slipped on the ice as they moved away from the Store. Caz looked back and saw that the front of it was seamed and thick with ice, the old sign frozen. It looked as dead as everything else. Yet inside there was warmth and life.

She had to keep her hope alive.

It was hard to find a way along the street. Glaciers of ice had frozen into cliffs and slabs, some as high as the buildings. They were heaped over each other in a jagged, lethal jumble.

Caz and Will had to climb and pull each other up, looking for cracks they could slither and crawl through. In some places they couldn't move without slipping back, and they had to hammer in small metal pegs for something to hold onto.

And the cold seemed to get worse.

They worked their way along the street until they came to a place where four roads met. They sat on the ice to catch their breath. Caz stared around.

Traffic lights – she remembered those. Red and green and amber. Now they were cased in ice, and below them the roof of a small car made a black frosty platform. Everything was sealed and silent, the ice filling the crossroads. From where she sat, Caz could touch the upstairs windows of the buildings.

Will stood tall on the ice. He said what she was thinking. "No one could have survived this. We're alone out here."

"Someone must have," Caz said. "We can't be the only people left. This was a huge city. It had millions of people."

But there was no sign of those people. The icy silence lay all around them. The sky above was clear and blue.

Only the wind moved. It whistled and echoed down between the dark walls of the city.

"Come on." Will turned. "We have to find some shelter. Which way?"

"West," Caz said.

"Why so sure?"

"Because that thing I saw was in the west."

Will was silent. "Caz," he said at last. "Listen. Don't get fixed on that. It might just have been ..."

"I saw it." Her voice was stubborn. "I know it was there." And yet she was scared now, in this cold and empty place. Scared that she had imagined that silver flicker of movement, that wink of red light.

They started moving again. The road west led deep into a district of high office blocks, past rows of trees dead and black with frost. Their shadows blocked the sun and lay dark blue on the ice. As she passed under them, Caz looked up and thought they were like giants defeated in some terrible battle. The wind hummed in their thin branches.

The only other sound was the scrape and clatter of Caz's boots, and the chink of the ice hammer.

They made steady progress as they got into a pattern with the ice hammer and ice hooks, but at the end of the last block they stopped and stared in dismay.

The river!

At least it had been a river, long ago.

Now it was a desert of frozen blocks and smashed chunks of ice, the surface cracked and furrowed. Boats and cranes were embedded in it.

"We'll have to use the bridge," Will muttered.

Caz looked at him. Under the fur hood of his jacket, his face glowed and his eyes were bright. He breathed out a cloud of frost.

"You like this, don't you?" she said.

Will grinned. "I feel alive, Caz. It's exciting, and it's real! Think how many years we've been locked up in the Store, when all this was out here!"

Caz nodded. She was moved by it, too. But she knew that there was nothing here to eat and nowhere to shelter when it got dark. And, worse, what if they were not alone?

Soon the street became a stone bridge over the frozen river. Caz and Will climbed out on it, feeling tiny and exposed away from the shelter of the buildings' high walls. But half way across they had to stop.

A great crack had opened in the roadway of the bridge. A lorry hung half off and half on. Its windscreen was smashed and its front seat was dusted with snow.

Far below, the frozen river lay like jagged teeth.

The gap between the two sides of the bridge was more than two metres wide.

"We'll never get over that," Caz said.

Will took off his pack and started to unwind rope from it. "We have to try," he said.

Chapter 5

River

Will hammered an ice hook hard into the ice and threaded the rope through it. He took the end of the rope and tied it in a loop around his waist.

Caz watched him, amazed that he knew how to do all this. She was bitterly cold. She ate a handful of dried apricots and drank some water.

"Ready?" Will said.

She nodded. "Yes, but what are you going to do?"

"Jump it."

She stared at him, appalled. "What if you fall?"

"The rope will hold me. If I fall I'll climb back up or let myself drop to the surface of the river."

It sounded like a crazy plan to Caz. "You'll never climb back up."

"That's what you think," Will said with a shrug. "I spent hours in the gym at the Store. I reckon I could."

Caz realised that was true. There was a staff gym in the basement at Murphy's and only Will had ever bothered to go down there and use it. Him and the Triplets, who sometimes hung out there, lifting weights and admiring one another's muscles.

Now Will took a few steps back and looked at the gap.

"If you make it," Caz said, "how do I get across?"

"I fix the rope on the other side and a hand line, and you cross it. That's how Arctic explorers did it. I've seen pictures in books. Anyway. Here goes."

Before Caz could say "Don't!" Will had started to run. He slithered on the ice, but he raced faster and faster towards the gap and then he leapt, flinging out his arms.

For a second he seemed to hang in the air.

Then he crashed down.

Caz gasped.

Will clung to the edge of the bridge. The ice hammer was stuck in the ice, but his feet hung in empty space. If the hammer came out, he would fall.

All his weight was on the hammer. As Caz watched, it jerked and then bit by bit it began to lean.

"Will!" she screamed.

His hand shot out. He grabbed and slid.

The ice hammer moved.

Will let go of the hammer and dragged his body up until his chest lay flat on the frozen stone. His legs kicked. And then he was over, on his knees, on his feet.

He turned to her and raised his arms, ready to yell in delight. Instead she saw fear slide into his eyes as he saw what was behind her.

"Caz!" he yelled. "Look out!"

She spun round.

Four animals were crouched in a row on the bridge. Their tongues were hanging out and their eyes were yellow with intent.

Dogs.

On the long nights in the Store, the stories they had told one another had always been about dogs. Dogs gone wild, gone feral. Dogs that hunted in packs across the empty city.

If anything survived, they had known it would be dogs.

Caz took a step back.

The dogs watched her. The wind lifted their fur. Three were Alsatians – big creatures like wolves. The other was a small, savage-looking thing with bandy legs. A pit bull. It growled, its jaws heavy and wet with saliva.

"Don't move." Caz heard Will's anxious voice.

"I'm not," she said, without turning her head.

"If you turn they'll be on you!"

Caz knew he was right. But all she wanted to do was turn her back to the dogs and throw herself over that gap in the stone bridge, because the fierce, steady stare of the dogs was more terrifying than anything. Her heart thudded. Her nerves jangled with terror. She licked her lips. "Will, I'm going to –"

"Wait!"

Something whistled past her and thumped at her feet. It was the ice hammer.

"Use it," he yelled.

The dogs rose up. One of the Alsatians barked, and the others began to move forward. Their ears flattened against their heads. Their teeth glinted as they snarled, a low, deadly threat.

Caz grabbed the axe and lifted it up. The leather of the handle felt damp and rough against her gloves.

The pit bull moved forward on its powerful legs, its belly low to the icy ground.

Caz made a frantic swing at it with the hammer. It was small, but it scared her the most. But they would all attack her together. She knew that.

The dogs barked in fury. Teeth snapped at the blade.

Wild with terror, Caz swung the hammer again, then took a step back.

As one, the dogs sprang. Caz struck out with all her strength and hit something, and then she turned and flung herself out into the air, brave with fear.

For a moment there was nothing under her but air. Then she hit ice with a crash that winded her and made everything go black.

She slithered. "Will!" she screamed.

She was falling!

She smashed the hammer in as hard as she could.

"It's all right," Will gasped. "Let go!"

She couldn't. All she wanted to do was keep her eyes closed and hold onto the safety of that grip. Then a hand grabbed her arm and her eyes snapped open.

"You made it," Will said.

Caz stared at him. Then she rolled over and sat up. Her body screamed with shock and pain.

On the other side of the gap, the dogs snarled their fury. Blood poured from the chest of one of the Alsatians. The others stood at the extreme edge of the bridge, barking and savage, drool frosting on their teeth.

Will helped Caz up. "Let's get out of here," he said. "Before more come."

They left the rope and they ran.

The noise drilled into Caz's head. She had become so used to the silence of this city that the dogs' savage din seemed terrible. It made her want to hide, get under cover, crouch down. But the scramble over the other side of the bridge felt dangerous and exposed.

As they ran and slipped their way towards the cover of buildings, Caz looked up, sure she had felt some shadow fly over her. But the blue sky was clear, empty but for the faintest trail of cloud far on the horizon.

By the time they reached the buildings, the dogs were far behind. The barking stopped. Will turned. Four dark shapes slunk away into the shadows.

Caz was worried. "What if they go further down the river and cross?" she said.

"We'll have to pray they don't." Will looked at her. "That took some guts, jumping that without a rope."

Caz shook her head. "Pure terror more like. I was just … I've never been so scared."

Will nodded. A gust of icy gale whipped his hair and they both shuddered.

It was getting colder. The sun was low, slinking like the dogs behind the roofs of the buildings.

"It'll be dark soon," Caz said. "What then?"

They stood in silence as the icy wind hummed all around.

Chapter 6
Underground

An hour later, they were shattered.

Caz's gloves were so wet and cold that she couldn't feel her fingers. Her ears were numb with the bite of the bitter wind. She was falling over her own feet with weariness.

A few steps in front of her, Will plodded, head down. All his excitement at being out in the city had gone.

They both dreaded the darkness.

"Will, wait," she said at last, and ran to catch him up. "We need to find shelter. Now. It's late."

Will looked around. They had wandered into an older area of the city. Here the streets were more like alleys, crooked and steep. The buildings seemed ancient, trapped in their tombs of ice. Their upper storeys leaned over the street, hanging with icicles like rows of silver daggers.

"I know," Will said. "But I don't think we ..."

Caz grabbed him. "Listen!" she hissed.

A sound.

It seemed to come from far away, deep in the city. A strange, eerie rumble.

They fell silent as they listened, and the sound changed note. It became deeper, then faded away.

"What was that?" Will asked.

Caz shook her head. "I don't know."

"Ice moving? Falling?"

"Maybe. Maybe it was something else." Caz listened again, but now there was only the whistle of the wind around the broken houses, the bang of a loose door somewhere behind them.

Will rubbed his hair under the fur hood. Ice crystals had formed on his eyelids and lashes. His lips were dry and cracked. "What about going down there?" he said, and he pointed at a red and white sign on a wall on the other side of the street. It was blotted with snow, but Caz could still read it. It said, "Stanton Street Underground Station."

"Underground?" she asked.

"The transport system, remember?" Will said. "Trains in tunnels underground. Think about it, Caz. It wouldn't be so cold down there – there's no wind either. That must be where they are if there are people still alive! It's obvious."

Caz didn't like the idea. "It'll be dark," she protested.

"We've got torches."

"Yes, but ..."

Caz hated to sound pathetic, but the idea of what might be down there chilled her. All those stories she had heard in the Store hung about her mind, of rats and creatures gone mad. After the meeting with the dogs she couldn't just shrug them off. Some of them might be true.

Will was impatient. "What choice do we have?" he demanded.

The Underground station was behind a wide archway. When they had climbed over the ice that blocked it from the street they found a dim and echoing hall, floored with frosted tiles.

Light fittings and wires hung from the roof.

A spilled litter bin rolled in the wind.

"This way," Will whispered. "Stay close together."

He had a knife in his hand. He handed Caz one too. They stepped with care, but their feet were loud in the stillness.

The hall led to some metal gates, but they were bent and easy to slip past. On the other side was a tunnel, high and cold.

Will and Caz crept down the tunnel side by side. Their shadows slid along beside them, high on the curved walls.

There was no wind. The relief of that washed over them like a warm blanket.

"Better?" Will murmured.

The tunnel took his voice and played with it, turning and returning it.

Caz nodded.

She didn't like this place. She looked around at walls that had once been white. Huge adverts hung in ragged strips. They showed a woman's smiling face, a sleek black car, scraps of what looked like a beach in the sun. Things people had worked and longed for. Things that didn't exist any more. Caz looked along to where the tunnel curved out of sight, and thought of all that world, all those people, gone and forgotten. A world that could never be rebuilt.

"Wait." Will dug into the pack, pulled out a torch and clicked it on. She was amazed he had managed to steal the batteries from the Store, but as the pale beam circled the darkness ahead she frowned.

The floor was gone.

A great dark pit waited for them instead.

Will walked to the edge. There was a metal stairway going down into the shadows, the steps big and thick and covered with dirty drifts of snow.

"It's an escalator," Caz whispered. She remembered, with a sudden shock, how she had feared these long, long moving stairs when she was small, how she had cried and her father had carried her.

Her father! For a moment, his smell and face and laugh came back to her. Was her father out here somewhere?

If he was alive, would she even recognise him now?

"I think we should take a rest before we tackle this," Will said. "Maybe get some sleep. And then, in the morning, we can go down there."

Caz shuddered. She couldn't sleep here – it was impossible. Anything might crawl up out of the darkness. She looked around.

There was a door off the tunnel, and when Caz opened it she saw a room with benches and rows of pegs, perhaps a cloakroom for the people who had worked there.

"In here," she said. "Then we can block the door behind us."

They cleared the floor, rolled themselves in coats and blankets from Will's pack, and lay down. Caz curled up in the corner. She was hungry and her fingers hurt from the cold. She would never be able to sleep.

But in seconds she was lost in dark dreams, where a strange low rumbling sound ran under her like a deep river of lost voices.

When Caz woke, Will was sitting up in his bundle of blankets, eating tofu stir-fry from a heat-up can. "OK?" he said.

She rubbed her face. "OK."

But she wasn't OK. She felt restless and uneasy. The small room was like a cell. She wanted to move on.

"We need to get down that escalator," Will said.

Caz nodded. "But," she said, "if I did see something in the sky, then maybe we should stay on the surface."

Will kept on eating, silent.

"So you don't believe ..." Caz began.

"It's not that." Will looked up. "But you said yourself you might have imagined it. We haven't seen a single sign of human life in this city."

Caz wouldn't argue. But as they collected up the blankets and pulled on their coats, she was filled with a nagging fear at the thought of going down into that unknown world of darkness.

She wouldn't let him see that.

As they climbed down the huge, still steps of the escalator, Caz looked at the adverts on each side, for theatre shows and films, for art exhibitions and days out.

'What's it like now in one of the big museums or galleries?' she wondered. Were the mummies still lying in their coffins? Were the famous paintings by Vincent Van Gogh and Leonardo da Vinci still on the walls? Caz had never been to a museum or a gallery, had never seen a painting. Or a mummy. Only in the books in the Store.

At the bottom of the escalator, Will stopped. He switched the torch back on and flashed it around.

They saw a white-tiled tunnel, split into three arches. Caz crept through the central one and found herself on a bare concrete platform.

There were metal seats, bins, signs. There was a scatter of rubbish, some suitcases, a toppled display of leaflets. Clothes from a rucksack had been pulled out and someone had rummaged among them. Caz stirred at the clothes with her boot, picked up one of the leaflets. Will wandered to the end of the platform.

This had been where people had caught trains. Caz remembered it now – the darkness, the hoarse roar of the wind in the tunnels and then the sudden rattle of the train, its bright windows and hundreds of people rushing with bags and umbrellas and pushchairs.

All those people.

All those children.

Gone.

Caz noticed something glinting on the concrete of the platform. She bent and picked it up and flicked her torch on it.

It was a round silver pendant on a broken chain. It showed a man carrying a child on his back. On the other side were the words, "St Christopher."

Caz turned the words over in her mind, but she had no idea who he was. She slipped the pendant into her pocket.

Then she turned. "Will?"

No answer.

She couldn't see him.

For a moment she felt only terror.

Then he stood up from a dark corner and walked back to her. "Come on. Let's get out of here." His face was pale.

"Bodies?" she said.

"Yes. Looks like people tried to hide down here when the Star came … Let's go, Caz."

"Wait," she said. "Look at this." She raised her torch to the wall and he saw it.

It was a huge map that showed the whole network of the underground tunnels. Each line was a different colour, the stations small circles of red.

Will looked at it. "Not much help," he said. "It doesn't show how far apart the stations are and I know some tunnels went deeper than others. Some even went under the river …"

He stopped, and they both stared. The circle of light from the torch had moved to show them a great black sentence scrawled on the wall next to the map. It said, "Anyone alive make your way here." A black arrow led from the words to one of the red stations on the map. The station was called Mortlake.

"What does it mean?" Will muttered.

"That people are there!" Caz said. "Or were." Those words could be nine years old.

"Right." Will took out a notebook and made a rapid copy of the map.

As Caz watched, she heard a whisper of sound from the mouth of the tunnel. She turned and stared into its darkness.

"Let's go." Will was ready. He walked to the edge of the platform and jumped down onto the lines of the track.

Caz stayed where she was.

It was stupid, but she couldn't get rid of the feeling that a train might come, rushing with terrible speed out of the darkness.

But she knew that would never happen again.

She let herself down, landed on her hands and feet, and dusted herself off.

Side by side, they walked into the inky black arch.

Chapter 7
Mortlake

Caz and Will walked for hours in the tunnels.

At least it was warm. Soon they had taken off their coats and hoods. The temperature down here was mild, the air dry and musty. It smelled of oil and salt.

In a few places water had got in, and dripped down the rounded walls in a green curtain of damp. There were flooded sections that they had to wade through. One of them was as deep as Caz's waist, and they had to feel their way step by step in case of sudden holes.

All along the walls there were great pipes and cables, crusted with salts and rust. Caz looked up. Would it be possible to get this going again? No.

Even if there were survivors somewhere, the old world was gone.

Since the Blue Star had flickered in the sky, everything had changed. They were living on a new earth now.

"Another station," Will muttered, and he lifted his torch.

They had passed six of the deserted stations. Caz didn't like them. They were littered with rubbish and they felt far more haunted and desolate than the dark tunnels.

Will was looking at the map. "We have to change lines here," he told her. "There must be escalators down to a deeper level. Let's have a drink before we carry on."

Caz handed him the water. "Take it easy. We're running short."

They had already drunk one of the three bottles dry. They would need to find more soon, or go back up to the surface and melt ice. 'But what if the ice was toxic?' Caz wondered. Would it be safe to drink it?

They climbed up onto the platform and found a maze of tunnels. "This one," Will said.

"No." Caz pointed. "That one."

"How do you know?"

Caz shone the torch over the wall. There, in the same black scrawl they had seen on the map, were the words "THIS WAY".

"Not sure I like this," Will said. "It feels like some kind of trap."

"I know, it's weird," Caz said. "But we need to look."

They walked down the tunnel in silence. It led to another escalator, but this one was so steep it seemed to fall away at their feet and plummet into the dark. As she made her way down, Caz's legs hurt with the weariness of it.

Down and down. Deep into the blackness. They must be a mile beneath the city by now.

All of a sudden, Will stopped and looked back. "What was that?"

"What?"

He flashed the torch.

And they saw it.

Movement!

Something scuttled in the dark. It was there and gone in a flicker of shadow, so fast Caz wasn't even sure she'd seen it.

"A rat!" she hissed.

"Too big." Will flashed the light to and fro. No movement. The metal stairs were empty. He turned. "Come on. Let's get down."

They rushed now, leaping and jumping despite the danger. But it still seemed an age before the handrail evened out and they saw they were at the bottom.

They dashed away to the platform, and then down onto the lines.

Will set off at a near sprint along the train tracks. Caz followed, but just as they got inside the tunnel she turned and looked back.

"Will!" she gasped.

The platform they had just left was crowded with eyes.

They glittered in the flash of the torchlight. Hundreds of dark eyes, intent on Caz.

"My God!" In a panic, Will shuddered the torch into bright beams that leaped back from the walls. "You were right," he cried. "They're rats! But huge!"

Caz didn't wait. She grabbed his hand and they ran. They stumbled into the tunnel, and with a rustle of horrible, crisp sound the creatures moved too, streaming from the platform.

"They're coming after us!" Will screamed.

"Ditch the pack!" Caz yelled.

"What! But the food –"

"That's what they want!"

For a second, Will hesitated but then he stopped, struggled with the buckles and straps and flung the whole pack down. Then he raced after Caz.

They plunged into the darkness, slipping in wet mud. As Caz looked back, she heard rather than saw the swarm of rats find the pack. The tearing of their teeth into the canvas made her shudder. But not all of them had stopped. A dark sliver of creatures kept coming.

"Faster!" she panted.

Running was hard. Caz still had her pack. The water was in it and they couldn't afford to lose it. She stumbled and almost fell, putting her arms down elbow-deep into the filthy, muddy water. Will hauled her up. Something touched her leg – a cold, wet mouth.

Caz screamed, then kicked it away.

"Look! Up there."

There was a narrow ledge ahead, just above the water, close under the side of the tunnel. Caz scrambled up and pulled Will after her. It was almost too small to edge along, and she could see the dark swollen bodies of rats trying to slither up after them. Some fell back with a splash, but then with a scrabble of its claws a large one made it. And another after that.

Their eyes glinted in the dark.

Will edged on ahead of Caz, as fast as he could. His breath came hard and tense. Behind him, the wall was slimy and slippery.

Caz kept her eye on the rats. If they came closer she would kick again.

But they waited, and more and more of them slithered up onto the ledge. Soon there was a rustling crowd of claws and sleek fur and greedy, hungry eyes.

Caz kept the torch on them.

Will pulled her along another few steps and the ledge widened.

It grew into a platform, scattered with debris, the exits all boarded up. A derelict station, lost even before the day of the Star.

On it was a sign.

It said "MORTLAKE".

Will climbed onto the platform and stared round. The boards nailed over the exits were thick and firm. "There's no way out," he said.

"There has to be," Caz said. "This is the place."

"I'm telling you, there's not!" Will's voice was sharp with panic.

A rat nosed onto the platform. Caz kicked at it, but it just ran into the shadows. A soft squeal came from her left. They were already all around her.

And then she had an idea. She took out the St Christopher pendant she had found and held it up. "Help us," she said. "Protect us. Do some magic for us."

The pendant spun in the light from the torch. It reflected a shimmering ray down the slimy wall, across the wet stones, to a round iron grate in the floor.

"There," she said.

Will ran to it. "It'll be rusted solid," he said, but then he bent and grabbed hold of the handle and stared.

"Look at this!" he shouted. "It's been oiled!"

Caz came over.

It was true. The lid had been cleaned and oiled. Only a thin layer of dust and dirt covered it.

When had someone done this? Months ago?

A year?

Will didn't hesitate now – his gloom was all gone. He twisted the handle, hauled the grid up and stared down. A ladder, fixed to the wall, led into the dark.

"You first," Will snapped.

Caz wanted to argue, but he was right. It was her turn to go ahead. She shoved the torch into her pocket, swung herself onto the ladder and began to climb down. It grew darker and darker and soon she could only see shadows. Above her she heard Will yell, then a rat plunged past her as it fell with a squeal into the pit below.

A few scrapes followed, then a clang.

Darkness closed in.

"Are you OK?" she called.

Will's voice came down, faint and distant. "I had to shut it," he called. "To keep them out."

Caz nodded. They both knew there was no way back now.

They began the climb down together.

Chapter 8
Spiders

The ladder seemed to go down for ever. And, all the time, Will's boots scraped off rust that fell on Caz like crisp red rain. Twice she had to hang on tight and catch her breath.

Then, just as her gloves slipped on the rail, her boot touched solid ground.

Caz turned and flicked the torch on.

The beam showed a square room of grey walls, with a door. The door was open a crack.

A thin slot of darkness showed on the other side.

Will landed with a thump beside her.

They both stood silent a moment. Then Caz slid off her gloves and pulled the hood from her face. There was a strange warmth down here.

Will crossed to the door. He opened it some more and peered in, his face tense.

"Corridor," he said.

Behind him, Caz saw a light switch in the wall. She knew it would be useless, but still she snapped it down.

Lights!

They crackled on so suddenly that Will swore in fear and Caz had her knife in her hand before she knew what she was doing. The lights rippled all down the long corridor, and they saw it was lined with doors and noticeboards where ancient papers hung grey with dust.

"This is so deep," Will said. "I can't believe it's still got power!"

Caz shrugged. What worried her was the silence. It didn't seem like anyone was here now.

Will walked along the corridor. It was thick with dust, and Caz trod in his footprints as she walked behind him. There were no others. And yet a strange breath of air moved the dust, stirring it in spirals up from the floor.

The first few doors were locked, but then they found one that opened.

The room behind it was a bedroom. The bed had been slept in, the sheets and blankets disturbed, as if the sleeper had awoken in a frenzy and flung them aside.

Dust and cobwebs covered everything.

Caz gazed in awe at the masses of web-like white cloud all over the ceiling. "Look," she breathed.

Spiders.

In this place deep underground, they had survived in their thousands. And that must mean there were other insects too. As she looked, Caz saw ants on the floor, small clouds of flies dancing in the lights.

A rustle made Will turn. He pointed and Caz saw a cat-like thing dart under a chair, as if the light had blinded it.

"There's a whole ecosystem down here," she said.

Will nodded. "So where are the people?"

The bedroom told them little, but a few doors on they found a huge room, filled with banks of blank screens, desks, wiring, computer terminals that were dark and silent. The computers in the Store had shown only blank screens since the day of the Star.

"This is a bunker," Caz said. "Some sort of emergency HQ."

Will nodded.

There were phones too, rows of them – some white, some black. One was red.

Caz picked up the handset of the red one and listened.

Silence.

"Hello?" she said, her voice soft. "Is anyone there?"

A crackle.

A whisper of air.

Caz's fingers went tight on the handset.

"Caz," Will said. He was backing away from a mass of web in the corner. "Look at this."

Caz wanted to listen to the empty line. She wanted to call out. "Are you there? Is anyone alive in the world but us?" But she put the phone down and turned.

"What?"

"The people. I've found them."

Will's voice was a whisper. Caz came up behind him and saw a cocoon of cobweb. It was thick and dense, woven over and over and round and round a thing that lay in its centre. And then she drew in a sharp breath and put her hands over her mouth. She saw a hand.

Dry and brittle, but human.

The fingers were bent, the skin yellow.

Caz went cold.

"How long?" Will asked.

"Years, I reckon." Caz stepped back. "They must have died from the effects of the Star. All of them, even down here."

There were more. Behind the desk, crumpled by the door. Each was a web now of busy spiders, a nest of other lives.

Caz felt sick. She didn't want to see any more. She couldn't.

Will seemed spell-bound, but as Caz turned away he came too. He picked up some of the papers scattered on the desk. Caz did too. They were faded, but she could read them. They were army reports, weather reports, print-outs from astronomers and scientists all over the world.

"The Star," she said. "They knew it was coming."

Will looked appalled. "No way."

"Look at this." Caz pointed to a date on the paper. 23rd March 2018. "Three days before the Star came," she said. "It's a report from someone in New Zealand ..."

She read the words aloud.

"*Confirmed, repeat confirmed, readings of approaching anomaly. The object registers magnetic disturbance and radiation. It is approaching Earth on a radical trajectory.*"

They knew about it. And they didn't tell the people.

"They must have thought they could destroy it." Will stared at the useless monitors, the dead machines. "Must have thought they could do anything, with all this." He took her arm. "There's no one here for us."

Caz shook her head. "But someone drew those arrows."

"Yes, but it might have been years ago," Will said. "But there should be food, and water. They would have stockpiled it somewhere."

Caz didn't want to go looking for it. She wanted, more than anything, to climb up and out of this buried place and into the light again.

But Will was right – they had to find food.

They crept between the cocooned bodies and ducked under hanging webs to make their way back to the door.

When they were back in the corridor, Will pointed to a dark metal door. "Let's try that one," he said. When they got close to it they saw it had been forced. A metal bar still lay on the floor near by.

Caz edged it open.

It was a storeroom and it had been looted. It had held tons of food, but now the cartons were torn open, the freeze-dried goods spilled and trodden on the floor.

Caz pushed her way in and went straight for the water. It was in two huge tanks, and one was still half full.

"Is it safe?" Will asked.

"How should I know?"

"Then we shouldn't risk it," he said. "We've got enough water for now, and there will be ice on the surface. It's food we need now."

"We could take this." It was a heat-up tin of sweetcorn, still sealed. A bag of dried apricots, still by some miracle fresh. Caz piled them up in her arms. "And maybe this. And ..."

She stopped.

Will grabbed her arm in shock.

Together, without breathing, they listened.

Somewhere, a door had clanged.

And now, out in the corridor, soft and rapid footsteps were pacing towards the storeroom.

Chapter 9
Stranger

Will moved fast.

He slipped behind the door and had the knife ready in his hands.

Caz dropped the tins of food with a clatter.

The footsteps stopped.

Caz held her breath.

She saw a man.

Her body went rigid with terror.

He was a tall, strong man, wearing a dark uniform of crisp cotton and a neat tie. His hair was perfect. He had no weapons that she could see.

He was the first stranger Caz had seen since she was five. She took a breath. "Who are you?"

He looked at her, and at the food on the floor.

"This facility is off-limits to the public," he said crisply.

"What? Look ... don't you realise ..."

"This facility is off-limits to the public. You will leave now."

It was as if he hadn't heard her. His eyes were clear and fixed on Caz, and they didn't blink.

"Are you insane? Have you any idea what's happened to the world up there?" Fury boiled up inside her. She stepped forward and stabbed her finger at him. His perfect neatness and calm was all wrong. "We've come all this way ... and everyone is dead! And you ..."

"Caz," Will said. "Caz, it's no use. He can't hear you."

"You will leave now," the guard said, in the same level voice, "or I will escort you from the premises."

Caz stared.

She stretched out to touch the man's arm and gasped. Her fingers went right through his sleeve.

The man stepped back. "You will not attempt to interfere with this unit."

An alarm began to ring, a harsh howl that made Caz's head hurt.

"It's not real," Will said. He came round and stood beside her. "Caz, it's some kind of hologram."

For a moment Caz couldn't believe it, then she felt sick with distress. For a moment she had thought they were not alone.

Will grabbed the food. "Come on. Let's get out of here."

He walked straight through the hologram to the door. Caz followed. For a surreal moment, she saw the man's face close in on hers and then she was through him. She looked back and saw he had turned and was still watching them.

"You are attempting to remove Government property," he said. "Please return the items and you will be allowed to leave."

Even outside, as they ran down the corridor, she heard the flat, level voice, so real, so calm, as it advised her to stop and return.

But the alarms soon drowned him out. As Will ran ahead down the grey corridor, the howl of the alarm grew louder.

"Wrong way!" Caz yelled. "We're going too far in!"

He turned.

Too late.

A panel of steel slammed down in the corridor, and sealed the way back. Caz dropped the food, held up her empty hands. "OK," she yelled. "OK. Look! We're not stealing anything."

The alarm howled on. "I don't think that matters!" Will yelled. He grabbed her hand and they ran round the corner. They saw two corridors branching off. Down the first one a panel slammed with a rusty clang.

"This way!" Breathless, Caz tugged Will into the only passage left. The sloping floor streamed with tiny silver insects, a flood of panic woken up by the clang of the door and the racket of the alarms.

Something hit the wall above Caz's head. She saw a blast of red light. Splinters of metal shot past her. "We need to get out!" she screamed.

There was nowhere to hide. Every door was locked. Will kicked one but it didn't budge. Caz looked back to try to see where the shots were coming from. She saw the hologram man form in a shimmer out of the air. He stood there and raised a small black gun. Another identical man shimmered out of the air next to him.

"Down!" Caz yelled.

They crashed to the floor.

The gun blast struck the door next to Will and blew it off its hinges. At once Caz was up and they were through, into a room so tiny she almost ran into the far wall.

"It's a trap!" she howled. "No!"

But Will was right behind her. And then she realised. She turned, saw the buttons on the wall, stabbed one at random.

The lift lurched.

With a smooth, clean hum it began to rise. They went up with astonishing speed, so fast that

Will slipped and Caz had to hold onto the wall to stay on her feet.

And then they were both laughing like crazy people, while rooms and floors flashed past the smashed door.

The lift stopped.

Caz took a breath and wiped her streaming eyes. "Where the hell are we now?" she said. "Are we at the surface?"

Will stopped laughing.

He peered out of the wrecked door. Then he turned back. "Caz. Take a look at this."

It was a vast cold room. A silent hangar. It was bigger than anything Caz had ever seen. And it was full of flying machines.

Chapter 10

Hangar

Caz and Will walked out into the hangar in awed silence.

The flying machines were of every size. Some were small microlights, others huge planes with jet engines. They were all covered with a fine dust, and as Caz walked through the ghostly shapes she felt the dust stir and rise under her feet. She coughed, then sneezed.

Will stooped under the giant wings of a huge cargo plane. "Why did they bring them all here?" he asked. "Was this a survival plan? To get people out of the city?"

"If it was, it doesn't seem to have worked." Caz touched a plane wing.

"They wouldn't have had time," Will said. "The Star killed everyone in an instant."

"We think that," Caz said. "But, Will, we don't know. We were in that Store, locked in. We never saw what went on outside."

The panic, the terror. Caz had never wanted to think about that. She turned, then stared. "Will! That's it!"

She recognised it at once. A small machine, sleek and silver grey, light and compact.

"The thing I saw flying, early the other morning. I swear it was the same as that!"

It seemed so long ago now, so faint a memory, but it had only been yesterday. The wink of red light in the sky, seen from a forbidden window.

Will was still for a moment. Then he found a ladder, dragged it over and climbed up into the cockpit of the machine. Caz turned.

Behind her were two huge hangar doors, locked and bolted. Under them, a thin line of white ice sealed the space.

The way out.

Will climbed out again and they sat at the base of the ladder to eat the last of the food and drink some precious water. Then they started work. Will got into the cockpit and tried every control. He searched among the vast piles of supplies and found oil and diesel that sent rank smells into the dim air of the hangar.

Caz worked on the doors. It took a crowbar and oil and all her strength to work the vast bolts back. But she was fuelled by sheer desperation and she did it. The locks were chained and she scrambled among the tools to find a thing with a rotating blade that seared through the rusty metal like a knife through cheese.

Strange images came into her mind as she worked. In the Store, in the empty Travel department, there had been great posters on the walls. They showed travellers with wheeled cases and rucksacks coming down stairs from planes much bigger than these, always with a blue sky behind them. Exotic buildings rose in the background, and often when Caz was small and bored, she had crept away to that room and sounded out the names of the cities she would never see.

Rome. New York. Sydney. And her favourite, because it was sounded so faraway. Madagascar.

Could they fly there now? Were there people there, all around the earth?

When at last they hauled the great doors open and the bitter wind roared in, they saw that the sun had set and it was dark. They were on high ground, and the hangar doors opened onto a wide airfield lumpy with deep snow. Beyond the airfield, the dim outlines of buildings huddled, the silent city.

Somewhere in those buildings was the Store. It would be about time for the evening meal.

Caz stared, and the wind flicked tears into her eyes.

"Rather be back there?" Will asked.

She shrugged. There was no answer to that.

The truth was that there was a good chance that she and Will would die out here – they had known that ever since they'd left. And yet, Caz had seen the openness of this night, the glitter of the icy stars overhead. That was worth taking risks for.

"No," she said at last. "I'd rather be here. You?"

Will pulled a face. "I've had enough of Marky for one lifetime."

He was staring too, at the dark city. She knew he was as afraid as she was. But at least they were together.

"Right." Caz turned to Will. "Let's do this."

They climbed up into the cockpit and Will pushed the ladder away. There was just enough space for two people to sit side by side. When Will pressed the ignition, the small engine coughed and throbbed into life. The low, smooth hum was a comforting sound.

"Do you know how to fly it?" Caz asked.

"No, of course not. But I've gone through the controls – there are only a few. These things must control themselves pretty much – my dad used to say that planes flew by computer."

Caz nodded. "OK. Let's see what happens."

Will pressed a glowing green switch on the panel.

With a smooth motion, the plane began to move. It unfolded its wings, made a series of trial movements and then, almost before they had time to strap themselves in, it was lifting.

The plane rose just above floor level and hovered there a second with a series of pulses of light. Then it moved towards the door. Will gave a quiet whoop of joy. "This is amazing!"

Caz nodded. The plane tipped a little and then righted itself. It reached the open hangar doors and hovered outside. As the light pulses touched the snow, they changed – the colour deepened to blue then dark purple. The note of the engine grew stronger.

"Here we go!" Caz muttered.

And then, almost without a sound, they were flying. They rose high over the deserted city, so that they could see the buildings drop away and become mere blocks against the white of the snow.

The wind was bitter, and it buffeted the little craft up and down. But then it steadied and the lights on the dashboard glowed green.

Caz yelled with the joy of it.

They were free of the dark tunnels. Free of the city.

Surely now they would find someone alive.

Chapter 11

Song

Caz had never imagined anything like this.

For hours they flew over the dark world.

Streets, parks, rivers, bridges passed below them, all locked and shimmering in a prison of ice. Once they saw a great amusement park, its twisting rides frozen, its huge Ferris wheel coated with icicles.

Caz and Will stared in silent wonder at the hills that rose to meet them, at winding valleys where only dead trees broke the icy surface.

When the sun rose behind them it transformed the landscape, lighting the snow in a rosy glow.

The sky turned blue, the clouds shimmered. Then Caz said, "Listen! What's that?"

It was a strange, beautiful sound.

Will lowered the hum of the engine and they heard it clearly.

It was song.

The song of a thousand shrill voices, of sweet notes and chirpings, of fluting phrases. Caz had heard it on DVDs in the Store, but never like this, never with such power and charm. As if the earth sang to meet the new day.

"Birds," she breathed.

They were sailing over a great wood. Will took the controls and they dropped to just above the tree-tops. A lake, oddly dark, passed in a flash. And then another.

"Strange," Will said. "That's not ice. It looks like it's …"

And then both he and Caz yelled. A line of white birds rose up from the surface – white birds with long necks and wide wings, their bills a blaze of gold.

"Swans! They're swans! But how …"

"The lake. It's not frozen." Caz pulled her gloves off, tugged the hood back. "And it's warmer here! Can you feel it? *It's warmer!*"

Spell-bound, they watched the great birds flap around the water, then settle again with a series of splashes. And Caz was sure now. On the banks of the lake were other, smaller birds, wading and picking in the mud.

"Insects." Will nodded at swirling clouds of gnats. "The whole place is alive!"

"But that must mean – if it's warm enough for animals … It must mean there are people."

Even as Caz said it, she saw them under the trees.

They had to be houses. They were small wooden structures and they looked rough and new. Will took the plane down. But no one ran out to look up at them. The doors of the huts stayed shut.

"What do you think?" Will said.

"We should land. They might be hiding. They might be scared of us."

He shrugged. "They might be, but I don't like the look of it."

Nor did Caz. There was something odd and sinister in the silence of those wooden shacks. But the vision of the swans was still joyful in her, so she said, "Let's see."

The aircraft spiralled down and landed on a lumpy hillside.

Caz jumped out. It was amazing! Real grass, full of tiny red and yellow flowers. Bees. Birds flitting past. She was so happy she turned a complete circle and feasted on the colour, the pale warmth of the breeze and the astonishing smells.

"The effects of the Star can't have gone as far as we thought, Will. There's life here, and the further west we go the warmer it will get."

Will said nothing.

"Will?" Caz turned, fast.

The cockpit was empty.

"Will. Where are you?"

Something touched her back. She gasped and spun, pulling out the knife, but already it had been knocked out of her hands.

Two men stood there, small and filthy and dressed in rags. One had some sort of weapon pointed right at Caz. Another had Will in an arm lock, one grimy hand clamped over his mouth.

"Well," one of the men said. "Seems we have a few runaways from the Settlement." He grinned, and Caz saw a line of black teeth. "And they've even brought us a plane."

Chapter 12
Settlement

The two men were fast and ruthless. They threw Will and Caz inside one of the huts and locked the door.

Then they went straight to the plane.

Bruised and dirty, Caz sat on the earth floor of the rough, dark hut. She pulled her knees up to her chin and watched Will prowl the stinking room.

She was bitter with disappointment. So these were other people! At last, after all these years she had found them, and this was how they were.

Dangerous. Ruthless. Thieves.

It was even worse than the Store.

"They'll take the plane," Will snarled. He was furious at himself. "The plane and the food and everything and we'll be left locked in here. If we're lucky."

Caz didn't want to think about what might happen if they were unlucky. Instead she said, "What do you think the Settlement is?"

Will stopped pacing. "What?"

"That's what the man said. 'Runaways from the Settlement.' What did he mean?" She looked up. "It must be where the plane I saw was from. Maybe these men are criminals sent away from there. Or –" Caz stopped.

Footsteps were approaching the door. She scrambled up.

The door opened and the smaller man stood there. He was holding a gun, black and with a slim muzzle.

"Well," he said. "Those Justices of yours thought they could exile us out here. But thanks to you two we're off to the City now."

"The City?" Caz stared. "But ... we've just come from there. It's frozen. Everything is dead."

The man laughed a hoarse laugh. "Yeah, right. You would say that. But we know the City's a paradise you Settlement people are keeping for yourselves. Stacked with food and shops and hotels and all that stuff from before the Star. You can't fool us. We know the truth."

The man lifted the gun and pointed it at Will. "Sorry. We can't leave you here as witnesses. The Justices might work out where we've gone. This has to be done."

His finger moved on the trigger.

Caz jumped at the man with a scream and at the same time Will dived to one side. A purple flash from the gun seared the wall behind him. Caz rocketed into the man with full force. He yelled and stumbled backwards, and then he fell and knocked his head against the door. The gun fired again, but by now Caz and Will were out of the door and running hard, over the open green hillside, up to the plane on the ridge.

As they ran, the other man came out of a hut, then raced towards them.

They reached the plane.

"Inside! Hurry!" Will yelled, but Caz was faster. She was already in the seat.

Will flung himself in.

"Start," he said. "Now!"

The controls lit. The engine hummed. The plane's wings ran through the series of rapid movements. A blast of purple fire seared past Caz. She ducked.

The plane began to move.

Caz looked out and saw the two men close by. One crouched down, raised the gun and aimed it. There was no way he could miss.

The gun levelled at Caz. She could do nothing but stare back at it.

And then, with a burst of sound, a knife of light fell from the sky. It was a silver plane. Bright and swift, it scorched down between them. All of a sudden, the two men were sprawled on the ground, the gun was broken and smoking, and the strange plane was shooting back up like an arrow into the sky.

Will whooped with joy.

"It's them! Will!" Caz screamed. "That's the plane I saw! It's them!"

As they shot up into the blue sky, Caz stared over her shoulder, scrambling round to find it again. And there it was. The silver plane banked out of a cloud and came alongside them, smooth and controlled and beautiful. Caz looked across and saw a man and a woman sitting in it. She raised a hand and waved at them.

The woman waved back.

Then a speaker crackled and a voice spoke. "Hi. You shouldn't be out here. This is too far from the Settlement. These are the criminal houses. It's not safe."

"Er, we're not ..." Caz shouted. "We've come from the City."

"The City! Really?" The man sounded astonished. "But there's no one's there."

"There are. There are people there. Alive." Caz spoke in a rush, thinking of Naz and Ade, Gwen and Fiona and even Marky, Stella and the Triplets. "They need help," she said. "They need to be rescued. We can show you where they are."

The speaker came back on and the woman spoke. "Follow us," she said. "We'll take you in."

"Where?" Will said.

"The Settlement. World's End. The Justices will sort this out."

World's End.

Caz grinned at Will. "How many people live there?" she asked.

The woman laughed. "Thousands. Everyone who survived the Star. You'll be safe there."

Her father. Would Caz's father be there, among those thousands? She was sure he would be, and she would find him. As they turned the plane and sailed through the pale blue sky she knew that the people in the other plane spoke the truth.

Everything would be all right now.

Below her the ice was fragmenting into fields of green and forested hills, just like in the pictures in Travel. And there, glittering on the horizon, were the spires and pinnacles and towers of a great Settlement.

The place she had dreamed of for nine long years.

The Settlement at the End of the World.

Will put his arm round her, and she leaned her head on his shoulder. And they were silent, staring out at their future.